CHRONOSHATTER

THE LAST EXPERIMENT

AHAAN MAKHIJA

STORYDEA
PUBLISHING

STORYDEA
PUBLISHING

7/22, Ansari Road, Darya Ganj, New Delhi-110 002
Phones: +91-11-40775252, 40775213
Web: www.storydea.com
E-mail: publishing@storydea.com

Published by Storydea Publishing

Printed & bound in India by Atlantic Print Services

Contents

CHAPTER 1

The Buzz in the Basement

Aarav was used to the sound of clocks. He liked them, actually. Mechanical ticks made sense; they were consistent, logical, dependable. They didn't yell at you for skipping P.E. or side-eye you in the canteen because you preferred resistor codes over cricket scores. No, clocks just ticked. But today, sitting in detention inside the abandoned wing of his school, Aarav realized he was hearing more than just the clock on the wall.

There was a hum. Low. Metallic. Constant.

It had started maybe five minutes ago, so soft that at first, he thought it was in his head. But now it pulsed, faintly but clearly, beneath the concrete floor.

The classroom smelled like rust and damp books. Water stains traced patterns on the ceiling, and dust clung to every surface like a second skin. The projector in front of him hadn't worked in years, yet Aarav had already taken off the back panel. Just because. Just to look.

His screwdriver was always tucked in his sock like a secret, sat neatly next to him. He didn't go anywhere without it. Some people carried pepper spray; Aarav carried tools.

He leaned forward, poked at the cracked circuit board inside the projector, then paused. There it was again.

The hum.

He straightened up slowly, turning his head, trying to locate it. It wasn't coming from the projector or the flickering lights above either. It came from below. Somewhere deeper.

No teacher had checked on him in the last thirty minutes. The corridor outside was probably empty. Most students didn't even come near this wing anymore, not since the new science block was built. This one had been forgotten except for detention sessions and the occasional janitor with a mop and a curse.

Aarav glanced at the door, then back at the half-dismantled projector.

"Screw it," he muttered, pocketing the screwdriver and slinging his bag over one shoulder.

He stepped out into the corridor, footsteps echoing faintly. The hum was louder here. Still subtle, but definitely there, like a machine buried somewhere deep underground, waiting.

He passed by Room B-9, then B-10. Cracked windows let in shafts of late-afternoon sunlight, casting dusty gold beams across the floor. At the end of the hall stood Room B-12, a door he'd never seen open in his three years at the school.

The sound intensified as he approached. His sneakers pressed lightly on the discolored tiles, but one near the door gave slightly under his foot with a soft click.

He froze.

A pressure sensor?

Aarav pressed down again. The tile sank just a fraction, but it was deliberate. He'd built enough small circuits to know what a trigger mechanism felt like.

Heart pounding now, he pushed open the door to Room B-12.

The air inside was stale and cooler than the air in the hallway. The room looked like a junkyard had exploded, with metal stools with broken legs, beakers coated in grime, bundles of wires dangling from the ceiling like forgotten vines. Posters of famous scientists peeled from the walls, their printed eyes long faded.

But the back wall … that was different.

At first, it looked normal, just another shelf crammed with dusty textbooks and broken glass jars. But as Aarav stepped closer, he felt it again. That shift in temperature. A subtle draft. A different energy.

The shelf was slightly off-center, and when he reached behind it, his fingers brushed cold metal.

He shoved the shelf aside. It groaned across the floor, sending up clouds of dust, and revealed a smooth, metallic panel bolted into the wall. It didn't belong. The edges were seamless, the surface a dark gunmetal grey. Right in the center was a strange insignia—two spirals rotating in opposite directions, fractured at the edges like they were caught in a glitch.

Aarav squinted. Definitely not any school logo.

He reached out, hesitant but curious. His fingertips hovered just above the surface.

Tick. Tick.

He snatched his hand back.

That wasn't a hum. That was a ticking sound. Sharp. Intentional.

He leaned in closer, careful not to touch anything. The ticking continued, now steady, maybe once every second. It sounded like a machine counting something down. Or up.

"What are you?" he whispered.

And then, without warning, the panel clicked.

Not loudly. Just a soft, mechanical click. But enough to shift the entire surface forward by a centimeter. Aarav stepped back, breath catching in his throat.

It wasn't a wall.

It was a door.

His brain started spinning faster than his mouth could catch up. What kind of door was sealed behind a shelf in an abandoned school room? Who put it here? Why was it ticking? And why, of all people, did it have to be him standing here now?

He looked around, half expecting someone to appear behind him. No one. Just the room. The buzzing. The silence wrapped in static.

His hands trembled slightly as he pulled out his phone. No signal. Of course not. He switched on the flashlight and aimed it at the edges of the panel. There were no handles, no hinges. It looked like it opened inward, maybe controlled electronically.

He could walk away.

He should walk away.

But Aarav's curiosity had always been louder than common sense. That's how you ended up in detention for fixing a teacher's microwave without permission. That's how you nearly electrocuted yourself trying to hotwire an electric scooter just to understand how its motor controller worked.

He took a deep breath and stepped closer again.

Something on the panel blinked. A red dot. Just once.

The ticking stopped.

Aarav swallowed hard.

That door wasn't just a forgotten piece of architecture.

It was listening.

And it had just noticed him.

CHAPTER 2

Blueprints and Broken Time

The door didn't budge that afternoon. No matter how long Aarav waited or how many times he pressed along its edges, the panel remained still. Whatever mechanism had caused it to shift had either shut down or gone dormant.

But it had seen him.

He couldn't get that part out of his head. The red blinks. The ticking. The sudden silence. Something or someone knew he had found it.

By the time the last bell rang, Aarav had already made up his mind.

He was coming back.

At exactly 1:38 AM, Aarav slipped out of his bedroom window, his backpack slung over one shoulder, flashlight, gloves, and a portable toolkit packed tight. He lived close enough to the school to make it on foot, and the streets of his neighborhood were quiet, lit only by the occasional passing headlight. As he scaled the side fence and dropped into the overgrown grass behind the science wing, he realized how quickly his heartbeat had risen—not just from the sneaking out, but from the anticipation.

This wasn't detention anymore.

This was a discovery.

The old corridor was darker than he remembered, the moonlight barely cutting through the foggy windowpanes. Every footstep echoed, making it feel like someone else was always just a few paces behind. He didn't stop. He couldn't. His head was buzzing with questions, with possibilities. Something was down there.

Room B-12 looked the same, but colder now. The tile near the entrance gave again under his foot.

Aarav pushed the door open, a flashlight beam sweeping across the wreckage of forgotten lab gear. The shelf had stayed where he'd left it. The metal panel remained exposed.

For a moment, he just stood there, unsure of what he expected. Then he walked forward and placed his hand flat against the panel.

Silence.

No ticking.

He pressed gently.

Click.

The panel shifted again, this time more confidently. A thin seam glowed faint blue around its edges, and then, without a sound, it retracted into the wall. A hidden hallway stretched beyond. Metallic, narrow, lined with grated floors and thin LED strips that pulsed like veins. The air that hit his face was dry and cold, heavy with the scent of old electronics.

Aarav stepped through.

The hallway sloped downward, spiraling once before opening into a vast underground chamber. He stopped, stunned.

It was a lab, but not like anything he'd seen in school or even online. There were long metal tables covered in dust and tangled cables. Glass domes lay cracked in corners, some filled with dark liquid long since evaporated. Journals were scattered everywhere, their pages yellowed and curling, as if someone had left in a hurry and never returned.

One wall was covered in old display screens, now dark. Another held shelves full of blueprints, all hand-drawn, rolled, and labeled with codes that didn't follow any conventional system.

His flashlight beam passed over the far table and stopped.

A single sheet of paper lay spread out, weighted by a rusted wrench.

Aarav stepped closer and picked it up carefully. The paper crackled in his fingers, but the title at the top was perfectly legible, printed in bold, spidery handwriting:

Chrono-Stasis Device: v0.9

His eyes widened.

Below the title was a detailed diagram of circular machinery surrounding a human figure, energy waves marked in concentric loops, and something that looked dangerously close to a time capsule. Notes ran along the margins in shorthand he didn't understand, but one phrase repeated several times: **"Temporal anchor unstable. Do not exceed 15 seconds."**

His mind raced. Chrono time. Stasis suspension.

A time-freezing device?

Was that what this lab had been building?

He didn't have time to finish the thought.

His wristwatch beeped.

Then glitched.

The seconds on the screen began to slow literally. The digital numbers stuttered, stuck between 1:58:42 and 1:58:43. He stared, frozen, as the world around him seemed to stretch like rubber. The flashlight beam bent slightly in mid-air. Dust particles floated motionless, suspended in the air like tiny stars.

The hum returned. Louder now. Deeper. Not beneath him, but around him.

Then, just as suddenly, it all snapped back. The numbers jumped ahead on his watch. 1:58:53. Aarav staggered slightly, grabbing the edge of the table to steady himself. The dust settled. The silence returned.

Ten seconds.

The blueprint's warning echoed in his head.

"Do not exceed 15 seconds".

What in the world had he just triggered?

He looked around the lab again, heart racing. There had to be more clues, more records, more evidence that he hadn't just imagined what happened.

But somewhere inside him, he already knew the truth.

He hadn't stumbled onto an abandoned lab.

He had stepped into a forgotten experiment.

And whatever it was, it hadn't been finished.

CHAPTER 3

The Missing Scientist

Aarav didn't sleep that night. He returned home just before 3 AM, hands still trembling, the blueprint rolled tightly in his bag, his thoughts unraveling faster than he could catch them. When morning came, he skipped breakfast, locked his door, and dumped the contents of his backpack onto the floor: blueprint, crumpled gloves, dust-covered flashlight, and a worn leather-bound journal he had swiped from one of the lab's steel cabinets.

It smelled of mildew and ink. Its spine was cracked, its cover embossed with faded letters:

Property of Dr. Ayesha Karim.

He flipped it open, half-expecting unreadable equations or technical babble. Instead, the first few pages were sketches, machine parts, diagrams, loops of waveforms annotated in looping handwriting. And then came the words.

"Time is not a direction. It is a question mark."

Every page he turned layered the mystery deeper. The entries weren't dated in a normal way; some were labeled with coordinates, others with phrases like *"After attempt 7A"* or *"Day -2 (again)"*. Some were almost poetic. Others read like notes to herself, warning and wondering at the same time.

By the fifth page, one line was underlined twice.

"Time isn't a line. It's a loop, and I've found the scissors."

He sat back, journal open on his desk. Who was Dr. Ayesha Karim? And what did she mean by "the scissors"?

The name felt familiar. Not from school exactly, more like something he'd overheard once, long ago. A whisper in the halls? A rumor buried under exam schedules and festival prep?

Curiosity took over. He dug into the old cabinet in the corner of his room, the one where his dad's outdated laptop still sat, collecting dust next to a pile of forgotten science magazines. Within minutes, Aarav was online, fingers flying across the keyboard.

It didn't take long.

A Google search brought up a few scattered mentions: an archived article from *The Times of India* dated 2004, a scanned academic paper co-authored by someone named

Dr. Ayesha K., and an old newspaper clipping buried in a digital library under "Disappearance."

He clicked it open.

"Brilliant Physicist Vanishes After Controversial Research Halted."

The headline sent a chill down his spine.

According to the article, Dr. Ayesha Karim had been a rising star in theoretical physics. A graduate of IIT Bombay, a published mind before thirty, and briefly, a science teacher at Aarav's school. She had joined for a short fellowship, working on experimental physics with "educational applications," though no one had ever clarified what those experiments were. Then, one day, she simply vanished.

Her lab was shut down. The wing she worked in Room B-12 was sealed. There was talk of obsession. Of instability. Some colleagues hinted she believed she could "step outside time." One local journalist had written: *"She claimed time had a weak point, like a zipper. And she was tugging at it."*

The image made Aarav shiver.

He scrolled further. Nobody had ever been found. No travel records. No financial transactions. No goodbyes. Just… gone.

He closed the laptop, staring at nothing for a long time.

His school and his classroom had held this secret for twenty years. Everyone must've assumed it was just another forgotten ghost story. A mad scientist in the basement. Typical school myth.

Except it wasn't a myth.

Because he'd seen the lab. The blueprint. The strange, shimmering glitch in time itself. He'd felt the way the world slowed, as if something ancient and mathematical had hiccupped right next to him.

He opened the journal again, flipping through the yellowed pages until one entry stopped him cold.

"If someone finds this, then the loop is already active. Do not trust time. It will lie."

His breath caught.

There were formulas below the warning, but Aarav didn't recognize half the symbols. Quantum notation, maybe. Spacetime metrics. He would need help decoding them if he even dared to ask.

Another page, near the back, had no formulas at all. Just one quote. Scribbled like an afterthought.

"They said I went mad. But madness is just seeing patterns no one else can."

Aarav leaned back in his chair, head buzzing. This wasn't just about time travel. This was about a machine built to *reshape* time, pause it, bend it, maybe even break it.

And somewhere inside this loop, Dr. Ayesha Karim had left a trail.

The question was: was she still out there?

Or worse, was she still *in* there?

CHAPTER 4

Echoes in the Hallway

It started with the corridor outside his chemistry class.

Aarav had just stepped out, rubbing chalk dust off his hands, when everything… paused.

Literally.

He blinked once. Then again. Everyone around him, dozens of students shuffling through the hallway, stood frozen in mid-motion. A girl had her hand halfway up in a wave. A boy balancing a cricket bat over his shoulder was caught mid-step, his leg hovering slightly above the ground. The chatter, the laughter, the scrape of shoes against tile is gone.

Not silence.

Just absence.

Aarav turned in a slow circle. No wind. No hum of lights. Even the buzzing tube fixture above him, which always flickered like it had stage fright, had stopped.

He took one hesitant step. The sound of his sneaker echoed far too loudly.

Then, with no warning, everything snapped back.

The girl completed her wave. The cricket bat hit the boy's shoulder with a thud. The hallway roared to life again, doors slamming, sneakers squeaking, backpacks bouncing.

No one else noticed.

Aarav stood still, heart hammering. He looked around wildly, searching for some sign that someone else had felt it, seen it. But everyone moved like nothing had happened.

And maybe, for them, nothing had.

That afternoon, it happened again.

Only this time, it was stranger.

During his history period, Ms. Thomas was lecturing about post-independence economic policies. Aarav knew the class. He remembered the exact diagram she drew on the board, right down to the uneven arrow she used to mark GDP growth.

But then, after the break, she gave the same lecture. Same words. Same pauses. Same diagram.

Some students looked bored. Others took notes. Nobody blinked at the repetition.

But Aarav sat frozen in his seat, eyes wide.

Something was looping.

By the time the third anomaly hit, an unexpected fire alarm during lunch, he was already on edge. The alarm blared for a solid thirty seconds. Students spilled into the field. Teachers looked confused. The principal barked orders over a megaphone. But the next day, when Aarav mentioned it, nobody remembered.

Not a single soul.

He even pulled aside Karan, the school's biggest gossip sponge. Karan swore on his limited-edition gaming mouse that there hadn't been any fire alarm this week.

That's when Aarav knew.

He wasn't imagining this. He wasn't sleep-deprived. He wasn't losing it.

The machine was doing something.

Back in his room that evening, he pulled the journal out again, scanning page after page until he found one marked with a jagged symbol in red ink. A warning.

"Loops may begin subtly. Fractures manifest as déjà vu, audio distortion, repetition, and memory gaps. They are not glitches, they are echoes."

Echoes.

That word clung to him like static.

Whatever had been dormant in the lab… it was stirring now. Bits of time were unraveling. Folding. Collapsing into themselves and then rebooting. Like a faulty circuit rebooting reality just enough to be noticeable if you were paying attention.

And he was.

For the first time, he felt something that hadn't touched him yet: fear.

Not fear of machines or strange science. Fear of not knowing what the limit was. If ten seconds could stretch time… how far could it go? Could it erase days? People? Him?

He looked down at his wristwatch.

Still working. Still ticking. But for how long?

He knew what he had to do.

He couldn't just observe this. He couldn't let things keep warping, hoping it would settle.

He had two choices.

Figure out how to control the machine or shut it down permanently.

He closed the journal and slid it into his backpack, along with the blueprint. This wasn't about solving a mystery anymore.

It was about saving time, literally from tearing itself apart.

And if he was right, those strange glitches were just the beginning.

Tomorrow night, he was going back into the lab.

And this time, he wasn't just going to observe.

He was going to start the machine.

CHAPTER 5

Code in the Chaos

Zoya Khan wasn't someone Aarav usually talked to.

She was the kind of person who didn't wait for others to catch up. Black hoodie, earbuds always in, fingers flying across keyboards like she was fluent in a different language because she basically was. President of the robotics club. Self-taught coder. Rumored to have hacked the school Wi-Fi just to block TikTok during exams. No one had ever proven it. Mostly because no one dared ask her directly.

But if there was anyone in school who could help Aarav figure out the madness unfolding under Room B-12, it was her.

He cornered her in the tech lab during lunch, notebook in hand, heart thumping.

"I need your help," he said, skipping the small talk.

She looked up slowly, one eyebrow raised. "You? Asking me?"

"I found something… weird."

"Define 'weird,'"

"Old lab. Hidden. Some kind of machine that messes with time. Blueprints. A journal. A shutdown system wired into the walls. A log I can't decode."

She stared at him.

Then blinked.

Then said, "Show me."

That night, they returned together.

Zoya didn't ask questions on the way. She just followed, flashlight clipped to her hoodie, fingers fidgeting near the laptop bag slung across her back. Aarav led her down the spiraled hallway, back into the cold underbelly of the school. The door hissed open again, smooth, like it remembered him.

Zoya stopped just inside the chamber, her eyes sweeping over the place.

"No one's been here for years," she murmured. "But someone built all this. Alone?"

"She didn't finish it," Aarav said, handing her the journal. "Or maybe she did and got… stuck."

Zoya flipped through the pages quickly, absorbing symbols and scribbles faster than Aarav ever could.

Then she moved to the old control terminal in the far corner. It was dark, but not dead. Aarav had never dared touch it. Zoya did.

"Manual interface," she muttered. "Completely offline... but not wiped."

She plugged in her tablet with a cable that looked older than either of them. Her screen blinked once. Then again. Code scrolled across it in slow waves. Aarav leaned over her shoulder.

"What are we looking at?"

"Log files," she said. "Lots of them. Sequential test runs. Numbered experiments, like time intervals. 'T-10'... 'T-45'... 'S-loop v0.8'. Most of them failed. But..."

Her voice trailed off.

She enlarged a section of the screen and pointed.

There it was.

A table of entries. Each row had a timestamp. Most were from years ago, 2002, 2003, 2004.

Then, one entry stood out. Highlighted in red. A recent date.

27/05/2025

Aarav's breath caught in his throat.

"That's... that's my birthday," he whispered.

Zoya didn't say anything. She tapped into the log details. It opened a sub-screen.

Test Subject ID: A-17

Temporal Sync Attempt: Incomplete

Status: Anomaly observed. Loop stable for 9.8 seconds. Manual override denied.

He took a step back.

"That's not possible," he said quietly.

Zoya looked up at him, eyes narrowing. "You've been inside the loop."

"No, I," He paused. Thought back. The frozen hallway. The repeating history lecture. The fire alarm no one else remembered.

He had been inside it. Not outside looking in. *Inside.*

His birthday wasn't just a random timestamp. It was the *activation date.*

"They logged me," he said. "Whoever set this up… they knew."

Zoya scrolled further, but the logs after that entry were encrypted.

"Someone's still accessing this system," she said. "Remotely, maybe. Or on a schedule."

"Can you trace it?"

“Not tonight. This tech’s older than my parents’ marriage, but it’s smart. The deeper I go, the more it pushes back.”

Aarav stared at the screen. At the line marked A-17.

It wasn’t just a machine reacting to him.

It had chosen him.

Or worse, it had *already used* him.

And now, whatever “loop” he’d stumbled into… it might not be done with him yet.

CHAPTER 6

Reverse Pulse Protocol

Zoya didn't sleep.

For two nights straight, she ran diagnostics on the copied logs, bounced old command lines through emulators, and manually decrypted buried code fragments. Aarav kept watch at school, making sure the hallway to Room B-12 stayed unnoticed. So far, the temporal "glitches" were small seconds repeating, sounds skipping, but they were growing more frequent.

On the third evening, Zoya called him over.

"I found it," she said, eyes bloodshot but focused. "The machine has a name. It was part of something called the Reverse Pulse Protocol."

Aarav dropped his bag and leaned in. "What's that? Some kind of project?"

"A failsafe," she said. "Karim built it for time *containment,* not travel. The goal was to freeze micro-timelines locally in the event of a global threat. Nuclear war, environmental collapse, pandemics, stuff they thought we couldn't survive."

Aarav frowned. "Like a stasis pod, but for cities?"

"More like… pressing pause on the fabric of time itself. A bubble. No aging. No decay. Just a suspended loop until danger passed. Only" she pointed to a flashing error line, "it didn't work."

The logs were clear. Initial tests had triggered spatial distortions. Local loops formed in unintended zones. Temporal echoing. Objects resetting. People repeat conversations without knowing.

One note hit hard:

"Fractures began expanding after 9.8 seconds. Full collapse threshold: 10km radius."

Aarav read it twice.

"If we restart it wrong."

"Yeah," Zoya said. "We don't just break time. We will erase it."

A heavy silence settled between them. Somewhere in the distance, a school bell rang. It echoed twice.

Zoya minimized the log and opened another file. "This next part is weirder."

A series of visual logs loaded grainy black-and-white footage from an overhead surveillance angle. A camera feeds from inside the lab. Each file was only a few seconds long. Most showed static or flashes of machinery. Then, she paused at one.

"Video A17."

The timestamp read **27/05/2025 03:12 AM**.

Zoya clicked play.

At first, there was darkness. Then, a flicker of movement.

A woman walked past the screen. Mid-30s. Braided hair. She wore a simple kurta. Carried a lunchbox. She smiled at something off-frame.

Aarav's heart stopped.

It was his mother.

Not a resemblance. Maybe not.

It was her.

Before the accident. Before everything. Walking like she always had, calm, distracted, humming to herself like the world could wait until she was ready.

Aarav lurched forward. "Pause it. Zoom in."

Zoya obeyed, silent.

He stared. His throat closed. "She's dead. That was… years ago."

Zoya clicked play again, but the loop only ran for five seconds.

She walked. Smiled. Stepped past the camera.

Then the footage snapped back to the same five seconds. Again and again.

He watched it four times before he looked away.

"Some kind of memory leak?" he asked, but his voice was hoarse.

Zoya shook her head. "That wasn't a memory. That was a capture. The machine pulled her into a fragment probably tied to your presence here. Emotional anchors. Quantum entanglement. I don't know the mechanics, but… the machine is *reaching* into your past."

Aarav swallowed hard.

"She was just… there," he whispered. "Like nothing happened."

"She's not alive, Aarav. Not *now*. That's a phantom, a loop. If we restart the core, it might pull in more."

He closed his eyes.

Five seconds. That was all he had. A glimpse. A flicker of something he had lost years ago.

But even in those five seconds, it felt like time breathed her back into the world. Like she had never left.

And now he had to decide whether to bring the machine back online, risking collapse… or destroy it.

Cut the wire.

Kill the hope.

Zoya didn't pressure him. She just closed the screen and said, "We're close. We need to decide before the system decides for us."

Aarav stood in the dim glow of the terminal, mind torn between science and grief, between the chance to fix the future and the temptation to relive the past.

And outside the lab, reality ticked on, increasingly unstable.

The clock wasn't counting forward.

It was counting down.

CHAPTER 7

Locked in the Loop

It started with the sound of breaking glass.

Aarav flinched, reflexes kicking in just as sparks burst from the overhead light tube above the machine's control panel. A bright flash lit the room for a second, followed by a high-pitched screech from one of the old terminals. Zoya ducked, shielding her open laptop. The lights overhead blinked twice and then surged to full brightness.

The hum that followed wasn't normal. It wasn't the low mechanical drone they were used to. This hum had *direction*. It crawled through the walls like it had a purpose. Then, just as quickly, it vanished, and the lab fell into total stillness.

Aarav stood still, muscles tight, waiting for something. A sound. A crackle. A tremor. But nothing happened.

He glanced at Zoya, who was already turning her screen toward him.

"I didn't press anything," she said. "I swear."

Before he could reply, the terminal next to them rebooted with a pop and displayed a flashing message:

TEST CONTAINMENT: LOOP-7A INITIATED

"What the" Aarav started, but then the lab shuddered again. The same light tube above them shattered again.

Zoya screamed this time, louder than before. Sparks fell in the same pattern as moments ago. Aarav reached out instinctively to grab her, but he froze halfway.

This had happened already.

Not just once. Not figuratively.

Literally.

Everything, every movement, every spark played out the same.

His mouth dried.

"We're looping," Zoya said. "This is a containment protocol. The machine's trying to stabilize something by locking us inside time itself."

"How long is the loop?" Aarav asked.

She checked her watch. "Just under seven minutes."

The alarm blared again. A high, painful shriek.

A second later, the room snapped back like someone had hit rewind and played simultaneously.

Glass. Sparks. Same scream. Same movement. Same static hum.

Loop two.

They were trapped.

By the fourth loop, neither of them flinched.

They had tried speaking at different times, breaking the pattern, changing minor details, but none of it worked. The second the alarm blared, reality reset. No warning. No escape. Even their digital watches were reset with each cycle. Only Zoya's manual stopwatch seemed to tick through the resets, each time starting back at zero.

"Why this loop? Why seven minutes?" Aarav asked after the fifth cycle, panting as the reset faded again.

"It's a quarantine window," Zoya said, flipping frantically through Dr. Karim's journal. "Seven minutes is probably the minimum cycle time the machine needs to assess and attempt recovery. If it can't stabilize, it loops."

"So it's trying to… fix us?"

"No," she said, "it's trying to fix *time*."

Zoya held up a torn page she had been saving, scrawled on it, in faint ink, were the final words from Karim's journal:

The final reset lies in the hour uncounted, where time forgets its name.

Aarav stared at the words. "That's a riddle."

"Exactly," Zoya said. "And it's the key to getting out."

Loop six.

They split up. Zoya returned to the terminal, trying to interrupt the cycle from the console. Aarav searched the lab for any kind of hidden override, something Karim might've installed as a manual release. The old testing chamber at the far end of the lab flickered irregularly. Wires hung like vines from the ceiling, and a portion of the floor still bore burn marks from some long-ago surge.

When the reset hit again, neither of them spoke. They just regrouped. This was starting to feel less like containment and more like *punishment*.

Loop seven.

Aarav sat down on the cold floor, staring at the phrase again.

"The final reset lies in the hour uncounted, where time forgets its name."

He closed his eyes and repeated it.

"Hours are named. Midnight. Noon. Sunrise. They all carry labels," he muttered. "What's uncounted?"

Zoya leaned back against the wall. "Maybe it's not an hour. Maybe it's a *place*."

He looked at her.

"You know where time doesn't get tracked," she continued. "The system monitors certain zones of the lab, but not all. Remember the blind spot?"

The corner.

The dead zone.

The one place the logs and surveillance feeds never covered.

Aarav jumped to his feet. "Let's go. Before the next reset."

Loop eight.

They ran to the corner chamber, a half-finished space shielded by steel cabinets and busted lab gear. Zoya's stopwatch ticked past the six-minute mark.

Six-fifteen.

Six-thirty.

Six-forty-five.

No reset.

They were in the eye of the storm.

The system didn't see them here.

The machine couldn't reach them.

Aarav crouched low, hand pressed to the wall.

"I think Karim built this deliberately," he said. "A safety net. A place *outside* the loop."

Zoya nodded. "Now we find the real exit."

She brushed aside a metal sheet and revealed a secondary panel completely analog. A brass keyhole embedded beneath cracked glass, with hand-etched words:

CORE OVERRIDE: AUTHORIZED ACCESS ONLY

It was real. Tangible. Mechanical. A backup plan left behind by a scientist who had feared the machine might one day trap someone else the way it had trapped her.

Zoya stood.

"We need the key."

Aarav exhaled, mind racing.

If Karim left this here, then the key had to be close or hidden somewhere only someone like him would understand.

Maybe not in the lab.

Maybe… in time.

CHAPTER 8

Fragments of Tomorrow

The deeper they dug, the more it made sense.

Not madness. Not an obsession. Not science gone wrong.

Dr. Ayesha Karim hadn't been trying to break the time.

She had been trying to save it.

Zoya uncovered the truth by hacking a series of encrypted logs buried in the oldest part of the terminal system data, so old that it had been labeled in Karim's handwriting rather than stored digitally. It took her nearly three hours to decode it all. And when she did, the pieces snapped into place like a final puzzle corner.

"She wasn't just trying to pause time," Zoya said, eyes wide. "She was trying to *store* it."

Aarav frowned. "Store it?"

Zoya turned the screen toward him. Schematics filled the display with complex diagrams of something Karim had called a Chrono Vault. Not just a machine, but a temporal archive. A place where seconds, minutes, even full days could be isolated and sealed like digital backup files of reality itself.

Karim's theory was radical but elegant: if the world ever reached an irreversible tipping point, climate collapse, nuclear war, mass extinction, the Chrono Vault could restore selected slices of history. Memories. People. Places. Not as illusions, but as recoverable, real moments.

"She was building a time-based survival system," Zoya whispered. "Not for herself. For all of us."

Aarav stared at the diagrams in stunned silence.

She hadn't failed.

She had almost succeeded.

Almost.

Zoya pulled up one last log that Karim hadn't written.

It was dated one month before the disappearance, and tagged with a different author ID: **VIRAJ-A17**.

Aarav leaned in.

That name. That code.

Viraj.

His eyes narrowed.

That was his father's name.

Zoya clicked the log open.

It wasn't a report.

It was a confession.

Ayesha, I've sealed the primary core. I can't let you finish it. You know why. He's already marked the system as tied to him now. If it activates fully, he won't survive the reset. I can't lose both of you.

I'm sorry. This is the only way to protect him.

Aarav felt the air drain from his lungs.

His father had worked on the project.

Not just working on it, but also helped design it. And then… stopped it.

Not because it was dangerous to the world.

Because it was dangerous to Aarav.

Zoya looked up, her voice soft now. "The ID match is exact. This isn't a coincidence."

Aarav couldn't speak.

He remembered pieces of it now. Bits of conversation. His father paced at night. Boxes labeled "University Archive" were hidden deep in the attic. His refusal to talk about why he left engineering.

It wasn't a burnout.

It was guilt.

He'd sabotaged the machine to protect his son and, in doing so, left it unstable.

That's why the loops were breaking out.

Why the machine had latched onto Aarav like a phantom limb.

It was unfinished. But I'm still aware.

Zoya cleared her throat. "There's more."

She pulled up one last schematic: a map of the facility, buried beneath layers of old architecture. At its center: a sphere.

"The Chrono Core," she said. "Still online. Still pulsing with energy. If there's a way to reset the loops, fix the containment failures… It's there."

Aarav stared at the map.

A glowing sphere sat three levels below the lab. Isolated. Shielded. But still alive.

"We go there," he said.

Zoya hesitated. "You sure?"

"If my father tried to shut this down to protect me… then I have to be the one to finish it."

Zoya nodded slowly.

"There's a line in one of Karim's notes," she said. "Something about inheritance."

She handed him the page.

Time cannot choose its guardians. But sometimes, it leaves echoes for the right hands to find.

Aarav folded the page, tucked it into his jacket pocket, and stood.

"Then let's go find the echo."

They moved fast. Through the spiral hallways, down through locked levels, Zoya cracked open with tools and code, until the walls began to hum differently. Not like before. Not static or broken.

This sound had rhythm.

Purpose.

They reached the door just past 1 AM. It was unlike anything else they'd see: a smooth obsidian metal embedded with circuits that pulsed soft blue, like veins under skin. A single symbol glowed in the center: two intersecting spirals, rotating in opposite directions.

The Chrono Core.

It was still awake.

Still waiting.

Aarav pressed his palm to the interface.

It recognized him instantly.

The doors parted.

Inside, bathed in soft light, hovered a perfect sphere floating above a platform of glass and wire, spinning slowly.

It wasn't just a machine.

It was a heartbeat.

And now, it was his.

CHAPTER 9

Chronoshatter

The moment Aarav stepped into the Chrono Core chamber, time began to splinter.

The sphere at the center of the room pulsed wildly now, its blue glow flickering between brilliance and void. Sparks leapt from exposed conduits along the ceiling. The ground trembled every few seconds, like the machine's heartbeat was syncing with something far more volatile.

Reality.

Zoya ran diagnostics on her tablet, frowning harder with each passing second.

"It's coming apart," she said. "The loops are bleeding out. Layering over each other. The timeline is… fraying."

Aarav stared at the sphere, mesmerized. Through its translucent surface, he saw motion shadows of moments, images flickering like memories: a paper plane flying, a teacher writing on a chalkboard, his mother humming in the kitchen.

The past wasn't gone. It was *stored.*

And now, it was leaking.

The control console behind the sphere lit up. Karim's final interface. The override system. Old-fashioned like a combination lock crossed with a piano. Meant to be read both by logic and intuition.

The message at the top blinked in soft orange text:

FINAL STABILIZATION REQUIRED

SELECT ONE PATH:

[PRESERVE PRESENT WORLD]
[RESTORE STORED TIMELINE]

Zoya turned toward him. "You can't choose both."

Aarav didn't respond.

He walked slowly around the sphere, watching pieces of his world fracture and loop behind its glow. A hallway at school replayed students walking through it again and again. The sun outside resets every three seconds. The lab shook again, heavier this time, a deep groan rising from below.

"Aarav," Zoya said, more firmly now. "We need to choose. The entire system's in flux. If we don't act"

"I saw her," he said, voice quiet. "My mom. In the stored data. Whole. Alive. Like she never left."

Zoya's shoulders dropped slightly.

"But if I restore that timeline…" he trailed off.

"You'll erase this one," she finished. "Everyone in it. Including us."

Another rumble hit the chamber. The glass floor fractured slightly beneath the sphere, webbing out like a spider's web.

"The restoration path will overwrite the present," Zoya said. "A perfect backup. But with no memory of this version. You won't remember *you*."

He turned to her. "Then what's the point?"

"To feel her again?" she asked softly. "Even for a moment?"

Aarav's hand hovered over the console. The interface waited. One key to reset it all. Another way to let it be.

He closed his eyes.

In the stored timeline, his mother lives.

But so does the mistake.

His father tried to save him by stopping the machine, but he couldn't. Time had already tied itself to Aarav. Every second he had lived was now entangled with every second he could erase.

And all of it was breaking.

Another surge of light cracked the sphere. Images began overlapping his seventh birthday *on top of* a school evacuation. A memory of his father soldering wires fused with a fire alarm blaring in reverse.

Too many timelines.

Too little time.

Then, an idea.

Not either/or.

Both.

Aarav grabbed the screwdriver from his pocket. The same one he always carried, the same one that started everything. He reached into the terminal's port and began unscrewing the casing.

"What are you doing?" Zoya shouted.

"Custom override," he said, prying it open. "The machine reads binary. Logic. Input. Command. But it wasn't built to read *emotion.*"

Zoya's eyes widened. "You're going to override the binary trigger with a hybrid key?"

"Not with math," he said, locking eyes with her. "With meaning."

Inside the terminal was an old circuit, fused but reactive. Aarav connected the journal page he'd folded earlier with Karim's final quote into the override reader.

Then, he pressed one finger against the biometric pad and whispered:

"I choose memory… not repetition."

The interface went dark.

For two seconds, nothing happened.

Then the sphere surged.

Light exploded outward, not violently, but *cleanly, as* if reality was being rethreaded strand by strand. Time slowed, then folded inward. The lab shimmered. Zoya stumbled back.

Aarav stood still, face calm.

He wasn't choosing one timeline.

He was stabilizing *this* one imperfection and all but threading into it the echoes of the past.

Not to rewrite it.

To remember it.

The sphere cracked but didn't collapse.

It dimmed. Then settled. A faint pulse remained, steady and alive, like a candle finally finding windless air.

The screen behind him blinked once:

SYSTEM RESET SUCCESSFUL

TEMPORAL LEAKS SEALED

CORE INTEGRITY: STABLE

Zoya exhaled hard. “You did it.”

Aarav turned toward her, but his face wasn’t triumphant.

Just quiet.

Resolved.

“You okay?” she asked.

“I think so,” he said. “I don’t remember… all of it.”

“But enough?”

He nodded.

Outside, the world had resumed. The sun shone. The timeline held.

The past hadn’t been rewritten.

But it had been *heard.*

CHAPTER 10

Aftertime

When Aarav opened his eyes, the lab was gone.

No flickering terminals. No hum. No glowing sphere. Just old concrete floors and cold morning air drifting through the cracked windows of Room B-12. The dust had settled. The metal shelves were back in place. Time, it seemed, had wiped away every trace.

Except him.

He stood slowly, scanning the room like someone waking up in a stranger's house. Nothing looked out of place. Yet everything felt… thinner. Like the room had been stretched and restitched.

Outside, the world ticked forward.

Students milled about the courtyard, laughing, arguing, alive in their ordinariness. A teacher called out a reminder about final exams. A janitor swept leaves near the science wing as if nothing extraordinary had ever happened beneath his feet.

But Aarav remembered.

Every glitch. Every echo. The seven-minute loop. His mother in a five-second shimmer. His father's warning is hidden in code. And Zoya, whose eyes once lit up in the blue light of a machine built to store time itself.

He passed her in the corridor.

She walked past him like she didn't know him. No recognition. No hesitation.

Just another classmate.

Zoya's timeline had been rewritten, like all the others. Their memories rearranged into cleaner versions. Safer. Lighter.

He was the only one the system left untouched.

The only one who still carried the weight.

Later that afternoon, he opened his locker and found something that hadn't been there before. An envelope. Cream-colored. Sealed in wax. No name, but somehow unmistakably meant for him.

Inside: a single handwritten note.

If time ever breaks again, let it be in the hands of someone who cares. A.K.

There was no doubt. Ayesha Karim had left it for him. Maybe before she vanished. Maybe in the final seconds, just before the collapse. Maybe impossible after.

Aarav folded the note carefully, as if it might disappear the moment he blinked.

He walked home slowly that evening. The sky above him seemed steadier somehow. More delicate. Like the world had just finished healing and hadn't quite settled into its new skin.

That night, he cleared his desk.

The books, the broken drone, the soldering kits. Gone.

He pulled out a blank notebook. A fresh circuit board. His father's old tools. On the first page, he didn't draw a weapon or a failsafe. No buttons to stop time. No triggers to erase it.

Instead, he sketched a bridge, a conceptual arc that could observe time without disturbing it. A system that could listen, record, maybe even learn. Not to trap the past. But to ask *why* it matters.

He stayed up till morning. No alarm. No loops.

Just the steady, quiet rhythm of time moving forward, second by second.

He titled the page:

ChronoShatter II: Not a Machine; A Conversation

And beneath it, he wrote something smaller.

A reminder. A promise.

Built not to save time. Built to understand it.

Outside, the sun cracked the horizon, golden and new.

Aarav stood at the window, eyes wide open, and smiled.

Because now, for the first time since it all began,

He wasn't afraid of time.

He was ready to talk to it.

About the Author

Ahaan Makhija is a young innovator, researcher, and storyteller whose imagination lives at the intersection of science and humanity. Currently a high school student at Springdales School - Dhaula Kuan, New Delhi, he has already earned national recognition in aerospace engineering and robotics, from winning the National Aerospace Challenge to filing a patent for a robotics diagnostic device. His projects often merge logic with emotion, data with design, and curiosity with compassion. For Ahaan, storytelling is another kind of experiment, one that tests the limits of empathy rather than circuitry. *ChronoShatter: The Last Experiment* is his debut novel, born from the late-night thoughts about memory, time and the cost of invention. Through it, he explores how science can be both a tool for progress and a mirror for the human heart.